SANT

A Note to Parents and Caregivers:

Read-it! Readers are for children who are just starting on the amazing road to reading. These beautiful books support both the acquisition of reading skills and the love of books.

The PURPLE LEVEL presents basic topics and objects using high frequency words and simple language patterns.

The RED LEVEL presents familiar topics using common words and repeating sentence patterns.

The BLUE LEVEL presents new ideas using a larger vocabulary and varied sentence structure.

The YELLOW LEVEL presents more challenging ideas, a broad vocabulary, and wide variety in sentence structure.

The GREEN LEVEL presents more complex ideas, an extended vocabulary range, and expanded language structures.

The ORANGE LEVEL presents a wide range of ideas and concepts using challenging vocabulary and complex language structures.

When sharing a book with your child, read in short stretches, pausing often to talk about the pictures. Have your child turn the pages and point to the pictures and familiar words. And be sure to reread favorite stories or parts of stories.

There is no right or wrong way to share books with children. Find time to read with your child, and pass on the legacy of literacy.

Adria F. Klein, Ph.D.
Professor Emeritus
California State University
San Bernardino, California

First American edition published in 2005 by
Picture Window Books
5115 Excelsior Boulevard
Suite 232
Minneapolis, MN 55416
877-845-8392
www.picturewindowbooks.com

First published in Canada in 1999 by
Les éditions Héritage inc.
300 Arran Street, Saint Lambert
Quebec, Canada J4R 1K5

Printed in the United States of America.

Library of Congress Cataloging-in-Publication Data
Papineau, Lucie.
Lulu and the magic box / Lucie Papineau ; illustrated by Catherine Lepage.
p. cm. — (Read-it! readers)
Summary: The tricks in Lulu's magic box can prevent nightmares, boredom, sulkiness, and much more.
ISBN 1-4048-1066-8 (hardcover)
I. Lepage, Catherine, ill. II. Title. III. Series.
PZ7.P2115Lu 2004

E]—dc22

2004024889

Lulu and the Magic Box

By Lucie Papineau
Illustrated by Catherine Lepage

Special thanks to our advisers for their expertise:

Adria F. Klein, Ph.D.
Professor Emeritus, California State University
San Bernardino, California

Susan Kesselring, M.A.
Literacy Educator
Rosemount - Apple Valley - Eagan (Minnesota) School District

PICTURE WINDOW BOOKS
Minneapolis, Minnesota

It's me, Lulu, with my lovely cat, Tilly.

This is my friend Billy with our teacher,
Mrs. Benson.

Here it is—my magic box! Inside, there are
fantastic magic tricks.

6

"Abracadabra! Peppers under arms! Let the magic happen!" I yell.

First Trick:
The anti-wrong-
side-of-the-bed
picture

Sometimes, I wake up on the wrong side of
the bed.

Nothing can make me change my mind:
I WILL NOT GO TO SCHOOL.

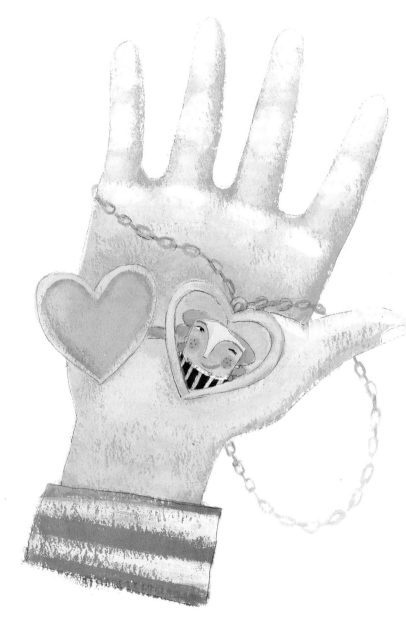

But when I look at the picture of Billy ...

Hurry! Hurry! My backpack!

Sometimes, I have super-extra scary dreams.

Afterward, it's super-extra impossible to fall asleep.

Luckily, Tilly sucks up the nightmare with the
magic straw.

Then my dreams are wonderful
until morning.

Third Trick:
The anti-boredom
cookies

Sometimes, I'm as bored as a gray sky.

I dream about having a baby brother.

Chocolate chips
Almonds
Marshmallows
Caram

Luckily, we have Granny's cookie recipe.

When the cookies are almost done, Tilly opens the window.

My three neighbors show up right away.

After five minutes, all the cookies disappeared!
So did my wish for a little brother!

Fourth Trick:
The anti-pouting
nose

Sometimes my parents disagree.

It always ends the same way—with Daddy
pouting in the living room.

Then I use the magic nose.

When Mommy sees Daddy like this, she
bursts out laughing.

When Mommy laughs like that, Daddy
laughs, too.

And when Mommy and Daddy laugh, the
disagreement is over!

In my magic box ...

I have plenty of other tricks waiting!

But the best one of all will never fit in a box.

"Abracadabra! Peppers under arms! The magic happens—with my Tilly!

More *Read-it!* Readers

Bright pictures and fun stories help you practice your reading skills. Look for more books at your level.

Bamboo at the Beach by Lucie Papineau

The Crying Princess by Anne Cassidy

Eight Enormous Elephants by Penny Dolan

Flynn Flies High by Hilary Robinson

Freddie's Fears by Hilary Robinson

Freddie's Fears by Hilary Robinson

Lulu and the Magic Box by Lucie Papineau

Mary and the Fairy by Penny Dolan

Moo! by Penny Dolan

My Favorite Monster by Bruno St-Aubin

Pippin's Big Jump by Jillian Powell

The Queen's Dragon by Anne Cassidy

Sounds Like Fun by Dana Meachen Rau

Tired of Waiting by Dana Meachen Rau

Whose Birthday Is It? by Sherryl Clark

Looking for a specific title or level? A complete list of *Read-it!* Readers is available on our Web site: *www.picturewindowbooks.com*